This book belongs to:

_____

Published by Ladybird Books Ltd
A Penguin Company

Penguin Books Ltd, 80 Strand, London WC2R 0RL, England
Penguin Books Australia Ltd, 250 Camberwell Road, Camberwell, Victoria 3124, Australia
Penguin Books (NZ) Ltd, Cnr Rosedale and Airborne Roads, Albany, Auckland,
New Zealand

This book is based on the TV episode "Top o' Big Tree", written by Scott Kraft,
from the animated TV series *Miss Spider's Sunny Patch Friends* on Nick Jr, a
Nelvana Limited/Absolute Pictures Limited co-production in association with
Callaway Arts & Entertainment, based on the Miss Spider books by David Kirk.

First published by Ladybird Books 2006
3 5 7 9 10 8 6 4 2

ISBN-13: 978-1-8464-6117-0
ISBN-10: 1-8464-6117-0

Printed in Italy

Miss **Spider's**
SUNNY PATCH FRIENDS

A Callaway Edition

Top o' Big Tree

David Kirk

The Sunny Patch bug scouts were having a meeting.

Mr Mantis said, "Tomorrow is our hike up the big tulip tree."

"That's the tallest tree in Sunny Patch!" Snowdrop said nervously.

"But if we reach the top," Squirt told her, "we will get our bug scout wings!"

The next morning, Mr Mantis limped into the Cosy Hole with a sprained thorax.

"I'm afraid we'll have to put off our climb," he sighed.
The little bug scouts were so disappointed!

Mr Mantis asked Miss Spider
to lead them.

"I'm coaching Dragon's
basketberry team today,"
said Miss Spider.

"Then perhaps Holley?"
asked Mr Mantis.

"I've never been camping
before," Holley said nervously,
"but I could try."

With Holley as their guide,
Bounce and Squirt raced
ahead.

"Hold your horseflies!" Holley
cried. "If you rush, you'll miss
all the wonderful sights."

"Yes," Snowdrop agreed. "This
branch's rings show that the
tree is very
old."

"Time for a snack!" Holley announced after a bit more climbing. "These tulip tree flowers are delicious!"

The scouts kept climbing.
The sky grew dim, and they
stopped for the night. Pansy
and Bounce started dinner.

"I'll hang our sleeping sacs,"
Squirt said.

"Wow, you bugs sure know
your camping lessons!" Holley
beamed proudly.

The stars looked brighter from high in the tree.

"Look! There's the bug dipper!" Squirt cried.

Soon the little bugs closed their weary eyes, falling asleep under the twinkling sky.

The next morning, Squirt and
Bounce felt very sore.

"Maybe we climbed too fast
yesterday," Holley said.

"I don't know if I can make it
to the top of the tree," Bounce
moaned.

"Climbing Big Tree is
a lot harder than I thought,"
Squirt panted.

"Come on, kids," Holley said.
"I know we can do it!"

Finally, Squirt and Bounce
were too tired to go any
further.

"Snowdrop, you and Dad keep
going," Squirt sighed. "At least
one of us should get bug
scout wings."

"No way," Snowdrop insisted.
"Bug scouts stick together."

"Why don't we stash our packs
in this hole?" Holley
suggested. "It would be easier
to climb without them."

After putting down their
packs, Squirt said, "I'm sure
I can get to the top now!"

"We are *s-so* high," Snowdrop
stammered. "I'm scared!"

"You can do it, Snowdrop,"
Squirt said, helping her up.
"Bugs scouts stick together,
remember?"

"We'll *all* be first to the top,"
panted Bounce.

Finally, the travellers reached the very tip of the highest branch.

"Great job!" Holley smiled, awarding each bug a pair of wings.

"But Dad," said Snowdrop, "you should have a pair of wings, too!"

Snowdrop had the honour of pinning wings on the newest scout in Sunny Patch.

At the top of the tree, the happy campers cheered.

This Ladybird book
belongs to

_____

J|1932272

A catalogue record for this book is available from the British Library

Published by Ladybird Books Ltd
27 Wrights Lane London W8 5TZ
A Penguin Company

2 4 6 8 10 9 7 5 3 1

© LADYBIRD BOOKS LTD MM

Printed in Italy

Here comes Dad

by Irene Yates
illustrated by Nicola Evans

Ladybird

Here comes Dad, he's ready to play.
What do you think he is today?

Dad is a troll – a tremendous,
trundling troll!

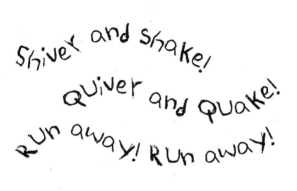

Shiver and shake!
Quiver and quake!
Run away! Run away!

"I'm a troll, a trundling troll!

waaaah!"

Here comes Dad, he's ready to play.
What do you think he is today?

Dad is a monster – a massive,
magnificent monster!

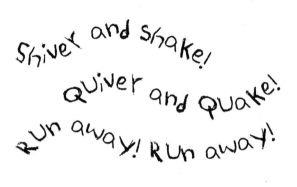

Shiver and shake!
quiver and quake!
Run away! Run away!

"I'm a monster, a massive monster!

Growwwl..."

Here comes Dad, he's ready to play.
What do you think he is today?

Dad is a crocodile – a creeping,
crawling crocodile!

Shiver and shake!
Quiver and quake!
Run away! Run away!

"I'm a croc, a creeping croc!

Snip! Snap!"

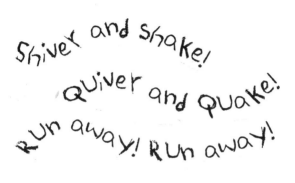

Here comes Dad, he's ready to play.
What do you think he is today?

He's a giant – a juddering,
gigantic giant!

Shiver and shake!
Quiver and quake!
Run away! Run away!

"I'm a giant, a gigantic giant!

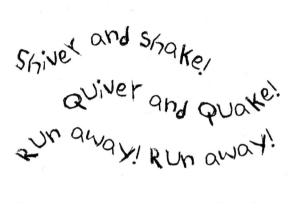

Grrrrrr..."

Here comes Dad, he's ready to play.
What do you think he is today?

He's a snake – a slithery,
slathery snake!

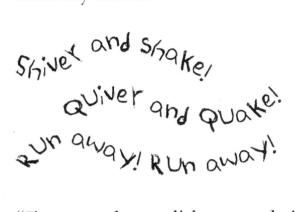

Shiver and shake!
Quiver and Quake!
Run away! Run away!

"I'm a snake, a slithery snake!

HiSSSSS..."

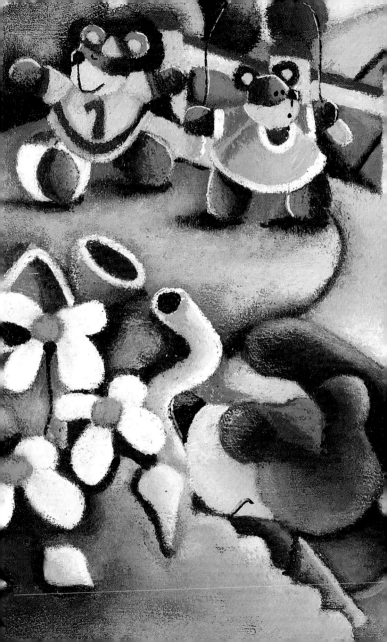

Here comes Dad, he's ready to play.
What do you think he is today?

He's a lion – a loping,
lolloping lion!

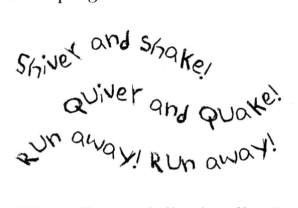
Shiver and shake!
Quiver and Quake!
Run away! Run away!

"I'm a lion, a lolloping lion!

Roar..."

Here comes Dad, he's ready to play.
What do you think he is today?

Is he a troll?

Is he a monster?

Is he a crocodile?

Is he a giant?

Is he a snake?

Is he a lion?...

...no, he's just Dad.

Lovely, lovely Dad.
Reading us stories, hugging
us tight, keeping us safe
all day and all night!